E   C
M

Moncure, Jane Belk.
  Play with a and t / by Jane Belk
Moncure ; illustrated by Jodie
McCallum. -- Elgin, Ill. : Child's
World ; Chicago, Ill. : Distributed by
Childrens Press, c1989.
  31 p. : col. ill. ; 20 x 24 cm. --
(Alphabet books)
  ISBN 0-516-06201-8 (Childrens Press)
: $8.95

  1. Alphabet.   I. McCallum, Jodie.
II. Title

MiMtcM 03 DEC 90   19263956   EYBAme   89-774

Distributed by Childrens Press,
Chicago, Illinois

Library of Congress Cataloging in Publication Data

Moncure, Jane Belk.
  Play with a and t / by Jane Belk Moncure ; illustrated by Jodie
McCallum.
    p. cm. — (Alphabet books)
  Summary: A brief tale emphasizing the uses of the letters "a" and
"t" in various words.
  ISBN 0-89565-505-5
  [1. Alphabet.]   I. McCallum, Jodie, ill.   II. Title.   III. Series.
PZ7.M739Pb   1989
[E]—dc19   89-774
                                                             CIP
                                                             AC

1 2 3 4 5 6 7 8 9 10 11 12 R 97 96 95 94 93 92 91 90 89

by Jane Belk Moncure
illustrated by Jodie McCallum

THE CHILD'S WORLD

ELGIN, ILLINOIS 60121

Starring the letters . . .

a and **t**

The publisher wishes to thank the letters "a" and "t." Without them, this book would not be possible.

This is little a

This is little

6

a and ✝ play.

What can we be?

This is little

May I play?

What can we three be?

Cat.

Play cat.

Do what cat can do.

This is little r

What can we three be?

Rat. Play rat.

Do what rat can do.

Play cat and rat.

This is little

May I play?

16

What can we three be?

Hat. A hat for rat.

What is that?

A rat in a hat.

What is that?

A cat in a hat.

This is little m

May I play?

What can we three be?

Mat. A mat for rat.

What is that?

A cat on a mat.

What is that!

Good-by, cat.

Good-by, rat.

Good-by, hat.

Good-by, mat.

29

and also

play with and

30

and

and

Can you?

31